Poems for Mental Clarity

Hatty Jones

Published by Hatty Jones, 2024.

This is a work of fiction. Similarities to real people, places, or events are entirely coincidental.

POEMS FOR MENTAL CLARITY

First edition. November 8, 2024.

Copyright © 2024 Hatty Jones.

ISBN: 979-8227849533

Written by Hatty Jones.

Poems for Mental Clarity

Life often feels like a labyrinth of thoughts—a maze where emotions, doubts, and distractions tangle and twist. In these moments, clarity can seem elusive, like a whisper lost in the roar of the world around us. This book is my offering, a collection of poetic reflections designed to cut through the noise and guide you toward stillness and insight.

Each poem is a small pause, a quiet invitation to breathe, to reflect, to let go. These words are not a solution, nor a final destination; they are signposts along the way, gentle reminders that clarity is not something to chase but something to uncover within yourself.

Mental clarity is not about emptying the mind—it's about connecting with the truth beneath the surface. It's about finding beauty in simplicity, calm in chaos, and strength in vulnerability. These poems are for anyone seeking that connection, anyone who needs a moment to step out of the rush and return to the present.

Take your time with these words. Let them be a conversation with your soul, a lantern to illuminate your inner world. In their quiet embrace, may you find not only clarity but also peace.

Welcome to this journey. May you uncover the quiet wisdom that already resides within you.

The Quiet Beckons

In the hush before the dawn,
When the world forgets its song,
Lies a space both soft and wide,
Where restless thoughts subside.
No ticking clock, no hurried pace,
Just the stillness of this place.
A breath, a pause, a fleeting sigh,
A moment where the self can lie.
The quiet whispers, calm and clear,
"Stay a while, for peace is near."
Within this still and tranquil space,
The soul regains its sacred grace.
Listen close; the quiet speaks,
Strength it gives to the weary and weak.
In its embrace, find what you seek:
A mind unburdened, a heart at peace.

Beneath the Noise

Beneath the clamour, soft and low,
A river's gentle currents flow.
The mind, though stormy, can be tamed,
Its whispers heard, its chaos named.
Each thought, a leaf upon the stream,
Drifting softly through a dream.
No need to cling, no need to fight,
Release them all, and find the light.
For in surrender lies the key,
To know what stillness means to be.
The noise dissolves, the heart expands,
And clarity unfolds its hands.
The world may roar, the winds may howl,
Yet within, a stillness prowls.
Seek it not, for it is near—
The quiet voice that calms your fear.

The Breath of Now

A breath in, a breath out,
Silences the mind's doubt.
No past to hold, no future to chase,
Just this moment's gentle grace.
The breath, a thread to guide the way,
Through tangled thoughts, where shadows play.
It whispers softly, "Here, be still,
Let go of striving, and just feel."
Each inhale, a chance to restart,
Each exhale, a balm for the heart.
The breath is present, strong, and kind,
A tether to the grounded mind.
No rush, no race, no need to flee,
The breath declares: "Simply be."
And in that truth, a world appears,
Where stillness soothes and quiet steers.

The Space Between Thoughts

In the gap where thoughts dissolve,
Mysteries of the soul evolve.
Between the words, between the lines,
A quiet power intertwines.
No clutter, no sound, no fight,
Only space that feels like light.
It asks for nothing, gives so much,
A healing presence, soft to touch.
In the stillness, truths take form,
Gentle winds before a storm.
It teaches us the art of rest,
The peace of silence manifest.
Not empty, but rich and vast,
A treasure found, a shadow cast.
The space between is where we find,
The beauty of a still, clear mind.

The Weight of Silence

Silence, heavy yet so light,
Wraps around the heart at night.
It presses softly, lingers long,
A space where nothing can go wrong.
No need for words, no need for sound,
In silence, healing can be found.
It is not absence, not a void,
But something deeper, pure, unspoiled.
It carries weight, but also lifts,
A paradox, a gentle gift.
Within its arms, the soul reclines,
And through the stillness, realigns.
Oh, let the silence cradle you,
Its whispers teach what's kind and true.
And in its weight, release the fight,
To find within a glowing light.

A Mind Like Water

A still pond mirrors the sky,
Reflecting truth without a lie.
It holds no ripples, knows no strain,
A tranquil mind, free from pain.
Like water, calm and crystal clear,
It harbours nothing, draws us near.
No need to hold, no need to bind,
A fluid grace that frees the mind.
Yet even water learns to flow,
Through storms and paths it doesn't know.
It bends, adapts, remains its own,
A gentle power, fully grown.
So may the mind reflect this art,
To flow with life, yet keep its heart.
A mind like water—calm, aware,
Unburdened by the weight of care.

The Gentle Anchor

An anchor holds, yet lets you drift,
A quiet strength, a steady gift.
It ties you not to weight or stone,
But to the self that feels like home.
When storms arise and winds pull tight,
The anchor whispers, "Hold the light."
No need to fight, no need to run,
Your center waits, the work is done.
The world may pull, the tides may rise,
But the anchor keeps you from disguise.
It grounds you softly, holds you near,
And whispers, "Peace is always here."
Oh, find your anchor, firm yet free,
And let it teach you how to be.
In stillness, strength will always grow,
A quiet truth the anchor knows.

The Whispering Wind

The wind does not demand or shout,
It moves with ease, it flows without.
A whisper, soft as morning dew,
A teacher of the subtle, true.
It does not stop, it does not stay,
But shows the path, then moves away.
No need to chase, no need to cling,
The wind is life—a fleeting thing.
And yet within its quiet sound,
A steady truth is always found.
It tells the trees to sway, not break,
It teaches rivers how to take.
Listen close, and you will find,
The whispers soothe the restless mind.
The wind, though quiet, holds its power,
A steady force through every hour.

The Shadow's Grace

Even shadows speak of light,
A quiet truth, a hidden might.
They dance and shift, they bend and play,
Yet guide the soul along its way.
In stillness, shadows gently show,
The places where the mind can grow.
Not enemies, but friends they are,
A map to where the brightest stars.
Do not fear the dark, my friend,
For it's where healing can begin.
The shadow whispers, "Rest awhile,
Your strength returns in every trial."
Through shadow's grace, the stillness shines,
A clearer path through tangled lines.
Embrace the dark, and you will see,
The light it hides is yours to free.

The Gift of Being

What is stillness but the art,
Of letting go, of feeling part?
No pushing forward, pulling back,
Just being here, no need to act.
The gift of now, the present true,
Is always waiting here for you.
No past regrets, no future fear,
Just this moment, crystal clear.
In being still, the mind finds grace,
A sacred, timeless, gentle space.
No need to fix, no need to heal,
Just be, and know the peace you feel.
The world will turn, the days will fade,
But stillness is a truth that stays.
A gift you carry, always near—
The simple act of being here.

Fragments of a Shattered Sky

Thoughts like shards of glass, they scatter,
In endless spirals, whispers chatter.
Pieces lost, yet pieces near,
A puzzle built of hope and fear.
The chaos reigns, a fractured light,
But clarity hides within the fight.
A breath, a pause, the fragments rest,
The mind reclaims its quiet nest.
Piece by piece, the whole returns,
Through focus, every fragment learns.
No need to rush, no need to flee,
Each shard a part of what will be.
Chaos fades, the puzzle clears,
The light emerges, calm and near.

Threads of the Mind

The mind's a loom of tangled thread,
A web of words both said and unsaid.
Knots of worry, strands of gold,
Stories fresh and stories old.
In the tangle, a path appears,
Through focus found and banished fears.
Each thread a thought, a moment caught,
A map to clarity long sought.
Pull gently now, untwist the fray,
Let purpose guide the strands today.
The web unravels, clear and kind,
A tapestry of the steady mind.
What once was chaos, torn apart,
Now forms a pattern, a work of art.

Through the Maze of Thought

A maze of thought, a winding trail,
Each turn a whisper, each choice frail.
The walls close in, the paths collide,
Confusion grows, nowhere to hide.
But focus walks with steady feet,
Guiding where the pathways meet.
A light ahead, a thread in hand,
Leads the way through shifting sand.
No maze too vast, no thought too wild,
For clarity comes when the mind's beguiled.
Each twist a lesson, each turn a test,
Until the journey finds its rest.
And in the center, peace is found,
The scattered thoughts now safely bound.

The Mirror Cracks

The mind reflects like a broken mirror,
Each shard a vision, none are clearer.
Pieces scatter, distort, and bend,
Yet hold a truth they cannot pretend.
Focus stands, a gentle hand,
To piece together what life demands.
A fragment here, a fragment there,
A story rebuilt with tender care.
The cracks don't vanish, they remain,
Yet beauty rises from the pain.
For in the broken, wholeness lives,
And what it takes, it always gives.
The mirror mends with light anew,
Reflecting now a clearer view.

The Storm Settles

A storm of thoughts, a wild gale,
Blowing reason far off trail.
Clouds of worry, winds of doubt,
The mind a tempest, spinning out.
Yet in the chaos, seeds are sown,
Moments of calm, their whispers known.
Focus gathers, the winds subside,
The scattered thoughts begin to guide.
The storm, though fierce, will always wane,
And clarity returns again.
Each gust, each howl, a passing guest,
That teaches the mind to find its rest.
The storm settles, the clouds recede,
And focus grows from every need.

A Symphony of Silence

A cacophony of thoughts, so loud,
A mind wrapped tight in mental clouds.
Each note collides, no rhythm clear,
A symphony of noise and fear.
But in the chaos, silence hums,
A quiet tune, its rhythm drums.
Focus listens, strains to hear,
The melody within the fear.
Each note aligns, the chords resound,
A song of clarity newly found.
The noise dissolves, the music grows,
The heart remembers what it knows.
A scattered mind, now steady, free,
Sings the song of clarity.

The Light of Order

Scattered thoughts like stars at night,
A cosmic web of fragile light.
Unbound, they drift, they twist, they turn,
Each seeking meaning they can't discern.
Focus rises like the dawn,
Pulling threads, both weak and strong.
Each light aligns, a pattern born,
Order rising from the torn.
The chaos folds into a map,
A guiding light from each mishap.
And what was scattered, far and wide,
Becomes the stars that light the guide.
A constellation, bold and bright,
Focus turns the dark to light.

From Fragments to Flame

The mind, a scattered ember's glow,
Each thought a spark, wild winds blow.
Ashes swirl, the fire fades,
Confusion rules the mind's cascade.
But focus fans the sparks to flame,
Breathing life into what remains.
Each ember gathered, fed, and stoked,
Becomes a fire, gently coaxed.
The blaze now warms, it does not burn,
A steady light from what we learn.
The scattered sparks, once wild, untamed,
Now glow with purpose, brightly named.
From fragments born, a fire alive,
Through focus, scattered thoughts survive.

A River Divided

A river splits, its currents fight,
Each pull a thought, each wave alight.
They crash and churn, they pull apart,
A torrent wild, a restless heart.
Yet focus is a gentle guide,
That calms the river, stems the tide.
Its hand, unseen, its voice so low,
Merges streams that cease to grow.
The currents blend, the waters flow,
The mind reclaims what it must know.
No longer torn, no longer pulled,
The scattered river, calm and full.
And in the quiet stream it makes,
The mind its steady rhythm takes.

The Art of Assembling

A puzzle scattered on the floor,
Each piece a thought, a hidden door.
The edges sharp, the image blurred,
A task too vast for spoken word.
But focus bends to gather all,
To place each fragment, large and small.
With every piece, the picture grows,
A deeper truth the process shows.
Not every piece will find its place,
Some are left for time and space.
But what remains forms something whole,
A quiet map to guide the soul.
From scattered fragments, something new,
Focus builds a clearer view.

The Veil of Grey

A mist descends, it wraps me tight,
Blurring edges, stealing light.
Each step uncertain, shadows grow,
The path obscured, which way to go?
Confusion whispers in the breeze,
A restless hum among the trees.
Yet through the haze, a voice I hear,
Soft but steady, drawing near.
"Do not fear the fog," it pleads,
"For in its depths are planted seeds.
Let stillness guide, let patience stay,
The light will find you, clear the way."
And as I pause, the veil recedes,
Clarity grows where doubt had seeded.

The Silent Guide

In the fog, the compass spins,
A battle neither loses nor wins.
The mind a maze, the heart unsure,
A weight too heavy to endure.
But quiet steps and steady hands,
Can navigate the shifting sands.
A whisper calls from deep within,
A place where clarity begins.
"Follow the breath, let go, be still,
Trust the strength of inner will."
The fog, though thick, begins to part,
And light ignites the weary heart.
The silent guide, though soft and small,
Becomes the path that conquers all.

Echoes in the Mist

The fog speaks not, yet echoes sound,
A million thoughts that twist around.
Each one a fragment, faint and slight,
They cloud the day and haunt the night.
Yet echoes fade if left alone,
Their power gone, their chaos flown.
The misty veil begins to lift,
A hidden treasure in its gift.
For what remains, when echoes die,
Is steady ground beneath the sky.
No longer bound by tangled fear,
The heart beats calm, the way is clear.
The fog retreats, the echoes rest,
And clarity reveals its crest.

A Lantern's Glow

Through the fog, a light appears,
A lantern held to calm my fears.
Its glow is faint, yet strong and true,
A guide through mist I cannot view.
Each step I take, the world unfolds,
The haze retreats, the story told.
Confusion yields to quiet thought,
The light reveals what I had sought.
The lantern's glow is always near,
A spark of hope, a shield from fear.
Though fog may try to blind the way,
The light within will never sway.
Through shadowed paths and murky skies,
The lantern leads where truth resides.

The Ocean of Fog

A sea of fog, its waves they crest,
The anxious heart finds little rest.
No stars to guide, no shore in sight,
Just endless grey in endless night.
Yet deep within, a compass spins,
Its gentle pull, the calm begins.
A single point, a whispered prayer,
Leads through the fog to open air.
The waves subside, the sea grows clear,
The shore emerges, steady, near.
What once was chaos now is calm,
The fog, a test that brought me balm.
Through storms and seas, I've come to know,
The way is lit by inner glow.

The Fog's Embrace

The fog surrounds, it holds me close,
Its tendrils soft, its whispers ghost.
An eerie calm, a world of grey,
I lose myself along the way.
Yet in the mist, I start to see,
The fog's embrace is guiding me.
Not to trap, but to conceal,
The truths I'm meant to slowly feel.
For in its arms, the rush is gone,
The world slows down, I carry on.
Each step unfolds a hidden truth,
A revelation from the proof.
The fog, though thick, becomes my guide,
And through its hold, I learn to stride.

The Clearing Path

A forest veiled in smoky grey,
No sun to warm, no stars to stay.
The path dissolves, the trees grow near,
Each shadow shaped by looming fear.
Yet in the mist, a rhythm grows,
A steady beat the spirit knows.
It pulls me forward, clears the way,
The dawn returns to light the day.
The trees withdraw, the grey turns blue,
The clearing shows a wider view.
For through the fog, the lesson clear:
The way is lit when hearts draw near.
What once was lost, I now can find,
The fog has sharpened heart and mind.

Through the Haze

A haze descends, it clouds the air,
Its weight a burden hard to bear.
The eyes see little, the heart feels less,
Each moment lost in emptiness.
But even haze, so thick, so vast,
Is only fleeting; it cannot last.
The sun behind, the light within,
Will pierce the fog where fears begin.
Each breath becomes a clearing breeze,
A whisper carried through the trees.
And as the haze begins to fade,
The open world is gently laid.
The haze dissolves, the vision clear,
And in its loss, the truth draws near.

The Fog and the Flame

The fog creeps close, it dims the fire,
It pulls at dreams, dulls desire.
A heavy cloak, a numbing grey,
It steals the light and veils the way.
But embers glow beneath the ash,
A spark too strong for fog to dash.
The flame, though faint, refuses death,
It burns within with every breath.
And as it grows, the fog retreats,
Its strength undone by steady heat.
The fire burns bright, the mist erased,
The way ahead no longer chased.
Through fog, the flame remains alive,
A beacon strong, the soul's revive.

The Edge of Fog

At fog's edge, the world feels torn,
A place where fears and doubts are born.
Each step unsure, each move a guess,
A wading through the boundless mess.
Yet just ahead, the edge appears,
The boundary of my hidden fears.
One step forward, the veil will break,
One breath deeper, the path I'll take.
The fog may linger, call me back,
But I have found the courage it lacks.
For through its depths, I've come to see,
The power of clarity lives in me.
The edge of fog is not the end,
But where new journeys can begin.

The Breath of Life

Each breath a thread, so soft, so thin,
Weaving the tapestry of life within.
A quiet rhythm, a gentle sound,
A steady anchor, ever found.
When chaos stirs and shadows rise,
The breath becomes a calm disguise.
A pause, a moment, a healing balm,
To steady the heart and find its calm.
No race to run, no goal to meet,
Just the simple rhythm of life's heartbeat.
Inhale the world, exhale the fear,
And let the moment draw you near.
The breath, a whisper, quiet and kind,
A gift of peace for the restless mind.
With every cycle, find your place,
And dwell within this breathing space.

A Pause in Time

The clock ticks on, its rhythm fast,
Each moment fleeting, none that last.
But in the breath, time bends and slows,
A sacred space where stillness grows.
A single inhale, soft and deep,
Can calm the waves, the storm can sleep.
A single exhale, strong and true,
Can clear the mind, bring forth the new.
The world may race, the hours may chase,
But here and now is breathing space.
No need for rushing, no need for speed,
The breath provides all that you need.
In this pause, the soul takes flight,
And time dissolves into the light.

The Rhythm of Rest

The body hums its quiet tune,
A pulse beneath the sun and moon.
The breath, a drummer, beats its sound,
A steady rhythm, profound, unbound.
When tension grips and shoulders strain,
The breath reminds to ease the pain.
A gentle rise, a soft release,
Each cycle bringing waves of peace.
No need to force, no need to try,
The breath sustains as moments fly.
Through every inhale, strength returns,
Through every exhale, the spirit learns.
This rhythm guides, this rest provides,
A haven where the soul abides.

The Breath Beneath the Storm

The storm above may howl and rage,
The mind a restless, spinning cage.
Yet in the breath, a quiet stays,
A shelter from the tempest's ways.
A single breath, a sacred start,
Can mend the cracks within the heart.
Though winds may lash and thunder cry,
The breath keeps calm beneath the sky.
Each inhale grounds, each exhale frees,
A steady anchor among the seas.
The storm may pass, the skies may clear,
But the breath remains, forever near.
It whispers softly, "This is your place,
The calm within the breathing space."

A Moment's Refuge

When the world grows loud, its colors bright,
And the soul retreats into the night,
The breath becomes a quiet room,
A sanctuary in the gloom.
No walls, no doors, no chains to bind,
Just open air for the restless mind.
A single pause, a fleeting still,
Enough to tame the climbing hill.
The breath asks nothing, offers all,
A gentle catch to break the fall.
It clears the noise, it holds the light,
A refuge in the darkest night.
This space, so simple, always near,
Provides the strength to conquer fear.

Breath by Breath

Breath by breath, the moment grows,
The tide recedes, the current slows.
No longer swept, no longer tossed,
The breath reclaims what had been lost.
Each cycle deepens, clears the haze,
A guiding light through endless days.
The smallest act, the simplest way,
To bring the soul into the day.
No need to plan, no need to think,
The breath is life's connecting link.
Its rhythm heals, its quiet speaks,
A source of peace that no one seeks.
Breath by breath, the soul finds grace,
Unfolding gently, space by space.

The Air of Stillness

The breath, unseen, yet always there,
A gift of life, a sacred air.
It asks for nothing, yet it gives,
A quiet force through which life lives.
In times of rush, in days of speed,
The breath provides the space we need.
A simple pause, a moment brief,
A world of calm, a source of relief.
No striving here, no race to run,
Just breath that softens what's begun.
Through every rise, through every fall,
The breath reminds we have it all.
Its stillness echoes, strong and wide,
A place of peace where fears subside.

The Bridge to Now

The breath connects, it draws a line,
From restless thought to the divine.
A bridge that spans from here to there,
A pathway made of open air.
When future looms or pasts intrude,
The breath restores a quiet mood.
It grounds the feet, it calms the mind,
It brings the present, soft and kind.
Each inhale builds, each exhale frees,
A moment strung on threads of ease.
The bridge is built, the way is clear,
To find the now, to hold it near.
Through breath alone, we cross the span,
And meet ourselves where life began.

The Breath of Letting Go

A breath in takes the weight we bear,
An exhale frees it to the air.
Each cycle holds a chance to shed,
The tangled thoughts within the head.
Let go of pain, let go of fear,
The breath will always hold you near.
It carries burdens far away,
And leaves you open to the day.
No force is needed, just release,
And find within the seeds of peace.
A breath in stills the stormy tide,
An exhale clears what dwells inside.
The act so small, yet vast its might,
To let things go and hold the light.

Infinite Space

The breath expands, it fills the chest,
A vast expanse where souls can rest.
No walls confine, no ceiling holds,
A boundless sky the breath unfolds.
Its rhythm flows, it ebbs and sways,
A dance of life through all our days.
Each breath a key to open doors,
To infinite worlds, to endless shores.
A single cycle, pure and deep,
Can wake the heart from restless sleep.
The breath, a journey, whole and free,
To endless space and clarity.
Step into this infinite room,
And let your soul escape the gloom.

Through the Lens

The lens of truth is crystal clear,
It shows the world as it appears.
No masks to wear, no lies to tell,
Just light and shadow where they dwell.
Through tangled thoughts, it carves a way,
To bring the night into the day.
It strips the fear, it lifts the doubt,
And lets the truth come pouring out.
The world, once blurred by noisy sound,
Becomes a still and solid ground.
No judgment calls, no shaded hue,
Just what is real, both false and true.
The lens of truth, so sharp, so bright,
Transforms the dark into the light.

The Mirror of Clarity

A mirror framed with fear and shame,
Reflects a face we cannot name.
It bends, distorts, and hides the real,
Replacing what we truly feel.
But hold it up, and see within,
A place where truths have always been.
The cracks may show, the flaws may stay,
But truth will light the hidden way.
Remove the veil, the filters fade,
No need for masks we've long displayed.
The mirror clears, it shows the whole,
The unvarnished self, the unbroken soul.
The truth is kind, though sharp it seems,
It holds the seeds of all our dreams.

A World Unveiled

The world unveils its vivid hue,
When seen through lenses sharp and true.
No longer dulled by fear's embrace,
Reality reveals its face.
The whispers fade, the noise grows still,
The truth ascends, it bends the will.
No need to hide, no need to flee,
The world is as it's meant to be.
The flowers bloom, the skies unfold,
Each color rich, each hue is bold.
What once seemed dark now shows its light,
As shadows yield to sharpened sight.
The world unveiled, so vast, so near,
A place of wonder, raw and clear.

Stripping the Layers

We wear the layers thick and tight,
They dim the day, they blur the night.
Each fear a fold, each doubt a thread,
A cloak we weave with words unsaid.
But truth's a hand that pulls away,
The lies we tell, the roles we play.
Its touch is firm, its purpose clear,
To bring the hidden self more near.
Beneath the layers, soft and worn,
Is where the truth is always born.
No need to hide, no need to shield,
The purest self will be revealed.
Stripped of doubt, the heart can sing,
A life unhidden, blossoming.

The Filter's Fall

The filter falls, its power spent,
It shatters lies, its veil is rent.
The truth emerges, raw and bright,
A spark that sets the soul alight.
No longer trapped by false disguise,
The self stands firm beneath clear skies.
No shadows cling, no fears remain,
The truth dissolves the cloud of pain.
Each step reveals a greater view,
The world transformed, both fresh and true.
No filter left, no mask to mend,
The honest self begins to ascend.
And in the fall, the heart will find,
The lens of truth frees every mind.

A Truth Uncovered

Beneath the noise, beneath the lies,
A quiet truth forever lies.
It waits for you, it hides in plain,
The part of self that will remain.
When stripped of doubt, when freed from fear,
The truth becomes a voice so clear.
Its tone is kind, its song is sure,
It shows the way to what is pure.
No need to seek, no need to chase,
The truth resides within your space.
Remove the weight, the chains of old,
And watch the truth's bright light unfold.
A truth uncovered, raw and bright,
Transforms the dark into the light.

The Whisper of Truth

A whisper calls beneath the din,
A voice of truth that comes from within.
It pierces doubt, it cuts the lies,
And clears the haze before our eyes.
Its tone is soft, yet firm and clear,
It drowns the noise, it soothes the fear.
It doesn't shout, it doesn't fight,
But gently guides the heart to light.
Through tangled webs of thought and sound,
The whisper leads to steady ground.
Its truth is simple, yet profound,
A quiet peace, a joy unbound.
The whisper waits, it's always near,
The truth within is yours to hear.

Unmasking the World

The world wears masks of shadowed hue,
Its truths obscured from every view.
But with the lens of truth in hand,
The lies dissolve like grains of sand.
The noise recedes, the echoes still,
And clarity bends light to will.
No longer hidden, veiled, or masked,
The world reveals the truths we've asked.
Each shape is whole, each line is clean,
The hidden threads now clearly seen.
The masks fall down, their work is done,
And what remains is just the one.
The world unmasked is bold, yet kind,
Its truths a gift for seeking minds.

Through Fearless Eyes

To see the world through fearless eyes,
Is to embrace what never dies.
The doubts may linger, the fears may play,
But truth remains, it doesn't sway.
The fearless lens reflects the soul,
Its cracks and flaws, its perfect whole.
No need for polish, no need for shine,
The truth it shows is always fine.
Through fearless eyes, the heart can soar,
The mind can rest, the soul explore.
Each moment seen, each color true,
Each vision clear, each angle new.
Through fearless eyes, the world expands,
A place that waits for open hands.

The Light of Truth

The truth shines bright, a steady flame,
It burns through doubt, it calls your name.
Its glow is warm, its touch is kind,
It clears the fog within the mind.
No shadow hides, no fear prevails,
The light of truth will lift the veils.
Its beam is sharp, it cuts the night,
And brings the hidden into sight.
What once was lost now stands in view,
A light that makes all things feel new.
It doesn't falter, it doesn't fade,
A beacon on the path you've made.
The light of truth will always show,
The way to self, the way to grow.

The Labyrinth of Thought

A labyrinth of twists and turns,
Each corner hides, each pathway burns.
The mind, a maze of tangled lines,
Of fears, of dreams, of shifting signs.
The walls are built from years of doubt,
A winding map I can't live without.
Yet through the fog, a trail appears,
A whispering voice to calm my fears.
I follow steps both slow and small,
Through endless paths, through rise and fall.
No map can guide, no compass steer,
The journey's mine to hold, to clear.
And as I walk, the maze unwinds,
The landscape shifts, the truth aligns.

The Meadow of Clarity

Beyond the storm, a meadow lies,
Its grasses green, its open skies.
A place where thoughts can freely grow,
Untangled truths begin to show.
Each blade of grass, a tender thought,
Each petal speaks of lessons taught.
The breeze moves soft, the world feels light,
A mental rest, a perfect sight.
No walls constrain, no shadows call,
Just boundless space to hold it all.
In this expanse, the mind can see,
The beauty of its clarity.
This meadow waits within the soul,
A healing space to make it whole.

The Forest of Reflection

The forest whispers soft and low,
With secrets only silence knows.
Each tree a thought, each leaf a dream,
Each shadow hides a hidden theme.
The pathways twist, the canopy tight,
Yet through its depths, a guiding light.
In every branch, in every root,
Lies wisdom ancient, firm, and mute.
The stillness hums, the echoes ring,
A symphony of everything.
The mind reflects, the forest clears,
Its leaves dissolve my quiet fears.
Within its arms, I find my way,
Through night and dawn, through dusk and day.

The River of Restlessness

The river flows, it twists and bends,
A restless path that never ends.
Its waters dark, its current swift,
A ceaseless pull, a constant drift.
Each ripple speaks of thought untamed,
Each eddy swirls with fears unnamed.
I step within, the chill runs deep,
The river steals, it doesn't keep.
Yet as I float, I feel the calm,
The water's touch, a healing balm.
The flow slows down, the surface clears,
And gently drowns my hidden fears.
The river shows what I must face,
And carries me to softer space.

The Mountain of Resolve

A mountain looms, its peak so high,
It meets the clouds, it scrapes the sky.
Its cliffs are steep, its paths are thin,
A climb that starts from deep within.
Each step is doubt, each ledge, a fear,
The summit seems so far, so near.
Yet through the climb, I learn to trust,
Each stone, each breath, each fall to dust.
The higher I rise, the clearer I see,
The strength that grows inside of me.
The air turns light, the view expands,
The summit reached with steady hands.
The mountain's climb was not in vain,
For in the struggle, truths remain.

The Desert of Doubt

A barren stretch, a land of sand,
Where doubts grow vast and out of hand.
No shade to find, no water flows,
Just endless paths where no one knows.
Each grain of sand, a fear untold,
Each mirage hides a truth of gold.
The sun beats down, the heat constrains,
Yet through it all, a strength remains.
The desert tests, it burns, it calls,
But teaches too, within its halls.
For through its trials, I have found,
The truths that hold me safe and sound.
And when I leave this barren land,
I carry hope, like grains of sand.

The Horizon of Hope

The mind expands, it stretches wide,
A landscape vast, where dreams abide.
The horizon calls, it glows with light,
It promises an end to night.
The journey there is not a race,
But steps to find my steady pace.
Each hill I climb, each valley low,
Brings me closer to the glow.
The past recedes, the future waits,
The horizon opens silent gates.
It beckons me to come and see,
The endless space of possibility.
The closer I draw, the clearer I find,
The hope that fills my heart and mind.

The Garden of the Mind

The garden grows in ways unknown,
Its flowers wild, its weeds full-blown.
The mind, a place of fertile ground,
Where seeds of thought are always found.
The blooms of joy, the thorns of pain,
The drops of doubt, the cleansing rain.
Each thought a sprout, each fear, a vine,
Entwined within this space of mine.
But with my hands, I clear the way,
To let the light return and stay.
The weeds will fade, the blooms will rise,
A garden thrives beneath clear skies.
Within this space, I start to see,
The beauty of the mind's wild tree.

The Cliff of Surrender

A cliff's sharp edge, a daunting place,
Where courage meets the fear I face.
The void below, the sky above,
A space where fear and trust both shove.
To leap requires a faith profound,
To trust the air will catch the ground.
Yet standing still will never show,
The truths that only leaping knows.
The mind resists, it pulls me back,
Yet whispers urge me to unpack.
And so, I leap, I fall, I fly,
And find the wings I feared to try.
The cliff becomes a place of grace,
Where I release and find my space.

The Sky of Possibility

The sky unfolds, it stretches vast,
A canvas free of all the past.
Each star a thought, each cloud a fear,
Yet all feel welcome, all are near.
The wind it whispers, soft and light,
Of dreams to chase, of endless flight.
The sky reminds, though doubts remain,
The heart can soar, it breaks the chain.
No borders here, no walls to climb,
Just endless space, unmarked by time.
The mind expands, it breathes, it grows,
The sky becomes the place it knows.
A landscape full of boundless grace,
The sky reflects the soul's own space.

The Compass Within

The world may spin, the stars may fade,
And leave me lost in paths unmade.
But deep inside, a compass turns,
Its needle points to truths it learns.
No map is drawn, no chart is clear,
Yet still it guides, both far and near.
Through doubt and fear, it finds the way,
A beacon for the lost to stay.
It whispers soft, "Trust what you know,
The steps will come, the path will show."
And though the winds may toss and roar,
The compass holds, a steady core.
Within its pull, I find my place,
A quiet strength, a steady grace.

The Needle of Trust

The needle sways, it dips, it swings,
Uncertain of the path it brings.
Yet trust is found in every turn,
A lesson deep I start to learn.
It leads through storms, it leads through calm,
Its rhythm like a soothing psalm.
No need to rush, no need to fight,
The compass knows both day and night.
Though trails may twist and fade from view,
The needle points to something true.
A guide unseen, yet always there,
It leads me past the world's despair.
Oh, compass wise, your path I'll take,
Through every trial, for truth's own sake.

A Guide Through the Fog

When fog descends and shadows play,
And every path seems led astray,
The compass calls with quiet might,
Its needle cutting through the night.
It doesn't shout, it doesn't push,
But holds its ground in every hush.
A steady hand, a silent guide,
It points the way where truths reside.
No outside voice can shift its course,
No storm can break its guiding force.
Through haze and doubt, its light remains,
A thread of hope in tangled chains.
Oh, compass, show me where to go,
When nothing else can let me know.

The Heart's Direction

The compass turns, it points inside,
To truths the heart has tried to hide.
No outward map, no stars to seek,
Just inner strength, though soft and meek.
It leads to places raw and bare,
Where dreams are born and shadows stare.
It asks me not to flee or fight,
But trust the journey's guiding light.
For every twist, for every fall,
The compass whispers, "This is all."
Each step I take, each choice I make,
Is part of what the soul must wake.
Oh, compass held in steady hand,
You lead me where I need to stand.

The North Star Within

No star to guide, no sky to trust,
The world around feels dark, unjust.
Yet deep within, a star will shine,
A light that's steady, calm, divine.
The compass points to where it glows,
A quiet north the heart still knows.
It doesn't fade, it doesn't stray,
But calls me gently through the fray.
When all seems lost, when hope is thin,
I turn to find the light within.
Its beam cuts through the darkest skies,
A reminder that the soul still tries.
Oh, compass true, your light I'll follow,
Through skies of fear and depths of hollow.

Pathways Unseen

The road ahead may split in two,
With no clear sign of what to do.
The compass spins, the choices vast,
It asks me not to dwell on the past.
Each turn I take, though blind, unsure,
Unfolds a truth that feels secure.
For paths unseen, though wild they seem,
Can lead to places born of dream.
No step is wrong, no trail in vain,
Each holds a lesson, joy, or pain.
The compass turns, it does not cease,
Its quiet pull a voice of peace.
Oh, guide me on through what's unknown,
For in the walk, the seeds are sown.

The Quiet Pull

When noise surrounds and chaos reigns,
When every step feels wrapped in chains,
The compass speaks in softest tone,
Its pull is gentle, yet my own.
No force, no shout, no urgent cry,
Just quiet trust beneath the sky.
It asks me not to race or flee,
But take each step deliberately.
The pull is light, yet strong as steel,
It guides the heart to what is real.
No matter how the world may spin,
Its quiet pull begins within.
Oh, compass, calm my restless heart,
And show me where the journey starts.

The Mapless Way

No map to guide, no path to trace,
Just endless roads, a boundless space.
Yet in my hand, the compass turns,
A faithful guide as the journey burns.
It doesn't need a map to show,
For paths unseen are where I'll grow.
Each step, though blind, reveals the way,
A brighter dawn, a clearer day.
Its needle points to what I seek,
Through valleys dark and mountains steep.
No map required, no lines to bind,
The compass charts the course I'll find.
Oh, trust the way that's born of soul,
For it will lead to something whole.

The Compass of Peace

When fear and worry cloud the skies,
And restless thoughts refuse to die,
The compass holds a steady line,
Its peace a gift, a truth divine.
It doesn't waver, doesn't stray,
But points the heart to a calmer way.
No rushing tides, no hurried pace,
Just gentle steps to find my space.
Through noise and strife, it softly speaks,
And helps me find the peace I seek.
Each turn it takes, each guide it shows,
Brings stillness where the chaos grows.
Oh, compass of my inner peace,
Let all the storms around me cease.

The Journey Within

The compass turns, it points to me,
To places I've been scared to see.
Its needle guides through lands unknown,
Where truths are planted, seeds are sown.
The journey isn't outward bound,
But inward, where the soul is found.
Through hidden fears and shadows wide,
The compass leads, it does not chide.
No rush, no race, no finish line,
The path it shows is purely mine.
Each step within, each truth revealed,
Becomes a wound, a scar, that's healed.
Oh, compass wise, your truth I'll follow,
Through light and dark, through joy and sorrow.

The Sky Unveiled

A sky so vast, so pure, so clear,
It wipes away each doubt and fear.
No storm to darken, no clouds to hide,
Just open space, horizons wide.
The mind, a mirror to the blue,
Reflects the calm, serene, and true.
Each thought a breeze, so soft, so light,
Each moment bathed in golden light.
No walls, no boundaries, just endless air,
A freedom found beyond compare.
Oh, cloudless sky, my soul you free,
A canvas vast, infinity.
In your expanse, I find my place,
A tranquil heart, a boundless space.

Beyond the Mist

The mist dissolves, the day breaks wide,
Revealing all the world inside.
The hills roll out, the valleys glow,
A path unveiled, a steady flow.
No fog remains to blur the view,
Each line defined, each color true.
The horizon calls with open arms,
Its quiet beauty, endless charms.
A mind unburdened, free to roam,
Finds in the vastness its truest home.
Each step is light, each breath is sweet,
Clarity rises to greet my feet.
Beyond the mist, the truth appears,
A shining path to calm my fears.

The Open Sky

Above, the sky extends so wide,
A peaceful dome where dreams reside.
No clouds to crowd, no storms to break,
Just endless blue, a tranquil lake.
The open sky, a quiet guide,
Invites the heart to set aside
The cluttered thoughts, the fears that bind,
To let the light embrace the mind.
Each glance reveals a deeper hue,
A sky untouched, a world anew.
The clarity within me grows,
A quiet stream that softly flows.
Oh, open sky, your truth I seek,
A world serene, a soul unique.

Endless Horizons

The horizon stretches far and free,
A line that calls, "Come walk with me."
No end in sight, no start to find,
Just open space to free the mind.
Its curve is soft, its reach immense,
A space untouched by walls or fence.
It whispers gently, "Look ahead,
Where light is born, where fears have fled."
Each step I take, the view expands,
A promise cradled in its hands.
The world unfolds, its beauty bare,
A boundless journey through the air.
Oh, endless horizon, draw me near,
And fill my heart with vision clear.

The Sky's Embrace

The sky wraps round in tender blue,
Its arms a sanctuary true.
No weight, no walls, no ties to hold,
Just open air, serene and bold.
Its touch is light, its song is sweet,
A refuge where the mind can meet.
Each cloudless stretch, each endless hue,
Whispers softly, "Start anew."
The clarity of sky and space
Brings calm to every hidden place.
The soul expands, the heart takes flight,
Through skies that glow with endless light.
Oh, sky so vast, my spirit rise,
To meet your truth beyond the skies.

A World Unfolded

The clouds retreat, the light breaks free,
Revealing all that's meant to be.
Each shape unfolds, each line appears,
A world reborn, dispelling fears.
The open skies, so soft, so bright,
Invite the heart to take its flight.
The weight dissolves, the mind takes ease,
A harmony flows through the breeze.
Each thought aligns, each dream takes root,
In clarity, the mind is soothed.
A world unfolded, fresh and bare,
A space of peace beyond compare.
Oh, cloudless skies, your calm I find,
A gentle solace for the mind.

The Clearest View

From peaks so high, the view extends,
A ribboned path that never ends.
The clouds give way, the air is bright,
A landscape clear in perfect light.
Each valley green, each mountain tall,
Stands open, free, no veil to fall.
The clarity of sight reveals
The beauty that the world conceals.
The mind reflects the view it sees,
A canvas wide, a flowing breeze.
Each breath is light, each moment pure,
The open sky a quiet cure.
Oh, clearest view, my guide you'll be,
To find the truth and set it free.

The Calm Horizon

The horizon whispers, soft and low,
"Follow me where the breezes blow."
Its edge extends, a golden thread,
A place where every fear has fled.
The sky above, the earth below,
Blend softly in horizon's glow.
No storm can touch, no cloud can mar,
This stretch of calm that feels so far.
Yet closer still, it draws me near,
Each step dissolves the weight of fear.
The clarity of skies so wide
Brings peace to what the heart denied.
Oh, calm horizon, let me stay,
Within your light, to drift away.

The Wind's Path

The wind, a guide through skies so clear,
Invites the mind to venture near.
Its path is soft, its voice is low,
It moves where open skies will show.
Through fields of light, through seas of air,
The wind creates a space to share.
No boundaries hold, no chains restrain,
Just endless skies where freedom reigns.
The mind becomes a soaring kite,
Guided by the wind's soft flight.
Through every turn, through every glide,
The world expands, horizons wide.
Oh, path of wind, so free, so true,
You lead my spirit to the blue.

Where the Skies Meet

Where the skies meet the endless sea,
A place of quiet calls to me.
Its edge extends, so vast, so deep,
A line where dreams and stillness keep.
The clouds are gone, the air is clear,
A space of calm that draws me near.
Each wave a thought, each breeze a sigh,
Each moment framed by open sky.
No weight to bear, no fear to hold,
Just space that feels serene and bold.
The horizon's line becomes my guide,
To walk where peace and light reside.
Oh, meeting place of sky and sea,
Reveal the calm inside of me.

The Unburdening

A weight I've carried, long and deep,
Through waking hours and restless sleep.
It clings to thoughts, it bends the air,
A shadow constant, everywhere.
But with a breath, the weight lets go,
A sigh that whispers soft and slow.
Each burden fades, each tether breaks,
A freeing path the spirit takes.
The sky unfolds, the heart expands,
The mind no longer caught in strands.
The weight dissolves, the soul takes flight,
Released into the boundless light.
Oh, weightless mind, at last you're free,
To simply rest, to simply be.

Letting Go

The mind is full, it overflows,
With fears it keeps, with pain it knows.
A heavy tide, it pulls me down,
A sea of sorrow where I drown.
But in the breath, the storm subsides,
The waves recede, the calm abides.
Each exhale whispers, "Let it fall,"
The burdens break, the weight turns small.
No need to hold, no need to fight,
Release the dark, embrace the light.
The mind, unchained, begins to rise,
Its freedom mirrored in the skies.
Oh, letting go, your gift I claim,
A weightless soul, a life reclaimed.

A Sky Unburdened

The sky holds nothing, free and wide,
No chains to pull, no need to hide.
It drifts, it flows, it simply is,
A model of what freedom gives.
The mind can learn this lesson too,
To hold no weight, to start anew.
Each cloud of worry, let it pass,
Each fear, a shadow on the glass.
And as the sky returns to blue,
The mind finds peace, its burdens few.
No tether holds, no anchor binds,
The soul ascends, the weight unwinds.
Oh, weightless sky, your truth I see,
To live is to be light and free.

Unshackled

The chains were forged of fear and doubt,
Each link a whisper I can't shout.
They held me fast, they weighed me low,
A quiet trap I'd grown to know.
But slowly now, the chains unwind,
Released by breath, by thought, by time.
Each clinking sound, a fading chord,
Each step a freedom long ignored.
The shackles break, the mind ascends,
To open skies where fear now ends.
The weightless air, it fills my chest,
A freedom earned, a life at rest.
Oh, unshackled heart, you find your song,
A soaring place where you belong.

The Feather's Way

The feather drifts, it knows no weight,
No anchor tied, no binding fate.
It floats where winds of chance may go,
A lesson soft, a truth to show.
The mind, so heavy, yearns to find,
The freedom of a feathered mind.
To lift the burden, shed the care,
And learn the art of open air.
Each worry left, each doubt released,
Brings lightness like a morning feast.
The feather shows the way to fly,
To claim the calm beneath the sky.
Oh, weightless mind, embrace the day,
And drift with life, the feathered way.

The Unseen Burden

The weight I bore, I could not see,
Yet felt its pull relentlessly.
A quiet ache, a pressing strain,
A burden held in heart and brain.
But as I breathe, I start to feel,
The grip it held begins to peel.
Each sigh, a tether breaking free,
Releasing what once buried me.
The mind grows light, the spirit lifts,
A treasure found in simple gifts.
No longer bound, no longer tied,
The weightless mind takes life in stride.
Oh, unseen weight, I let you fall,
And claim the freedom over all.

Through Open Air

The air invites, it lifts, it clears,
It carries off my heavy fears.
Each breath it takes, it softly steals,
The weight that endless worry seals.
Through open air, the burdens fade,
The clinging doubts are now unmade.
No tether holds, no anchor grips,
The weightless mind begins its trips.
Each step feels light, each thought is pure,
A gentle calm, a lasting cure.
Through open air, the mind is free,
To float where life's own winds decree.
Oh, airy space, your truth I see,
In weightlessness, I learn to be.

The Light Within

The light inside begins to grow,
As burdens cease and rivers flow.
The weight I carried, tight and cold,
Melts away as truths unfold.
The mind, once burdened, starts to shine,
Its glow expands, a light divine.
No longer dimmed by doubt or fear,
Its vision wide, its purpose clear.
The weightless state, a sacred space,
Where joy and hope begin to race.
The heart ascends, the spirit flies,
Its wings unfurled beneath wide skies.
Oh, inner light, your warmth I find,
A glowing path to a weightless mind.

The Wind's Release

The wind arrives, it lifts, it frees,
It carries weight like falling leaves.
Each burden caught, each doubt undone,
A freedom born beneath the sun.
The breeze, it whispers, "Let it fall,
You need not carry it at all."
It sweeps the mind, it clears the air,
Until no weight is left to bear.
The world feels light, the spirit soars,
The mind unlocks its hidden doors.
Through winds of change, the burdens flee,
And clarity returns to me.
Oh, weightless breeze, your truth I feel,
A mind unchained, a soul that's healed.

The Burden Set Free

The burden was a silent stone,
A weight I thought was mine alone.
It pressed, it held, it shaped my frame,
A quiet source of nameless blame.
But slowly now, I set it down,
A gift of freedom newly found.
Each step away, my body grows,
Each breath a space where calmness flows.
The stone remains, but not with me,
Its weight a thing I chose to free.
The mind ascends, the soul takes flight,
Unbound at last by heavy night.
Oh, burden set free, your lesson stays,
In weightless skies, I find my ways.

The Threshold of Quiet

Between the chaos, loud and wide,
And stillness where my truths reside,
There lies a space, both soft and strong,
A place where I can belong.
The noise surrounds, it pulls, it screams,
It weaves a web of shattered dreams.
But deeper still, a whisper grows,
A gentle calm the spirit knows.
No need to fight, no need to run,
The stillness waits when chaos is done.
It doesn't push, it doesn't plead,
But offers all the peace I need.
Between the noise and quiet's call,
I find the balance in it all.

The Echo's End

The echo rings, it fills the air,
A clamour fierce, beyond compare.
It bounces loud, it will not rest,
A noise that burdens heart and chest.
Yet as it fades, the silence grows,
A sanctuary the spirit knows.
The stillness speaks in tones so low,
A hidden truth begins to show.
Between the echo and its fall,
A voice arises, calm and small.
It teaches balance, patience, grace,
A tender, quiet, healing space.
Oh, let the echoes softly fade,
And bring me peace where stillness stayed.

The Crescendo and the Pause

The world erupts in waves of sound,
A deafening pulse, it spins around.
Each thought a chord, each fear a note,
A symphony that grips my throat.
Yet through the noise, the silence calls,
It hums beneath the crashing falls.
A pause between the loudest cries,
A steady rhythm softly lies.
The balance lives in every tone,
The harmony of all I've known.
Each beat, each rest, a bridge, a guide,
Between the worlds where I reside.
In the crescendo, find the still,
A place where time can bend to will.

The Whisper Beneath

The noise consumes, it wraps me tight,
It fills my days, it steals my night.
A restless buzz, it drowns the air,
A storm of thought beyond repair.
But deep beneath, a whisper flows,
A quiet strength the silence knows.
It asks for trust, it seeks no fight,
It holds the calm of endless night.
Between the noise and whisper's grace,
I find my breath, I find my space.
No need to choose, no need to hide,
Both chaos and stillness reside.
In their dance, I come to see,
The quiet is what sets me free.

The Edge of Silence

At the edge of silence, noise still roars,
It beats against my spirit's doors.
Yet just beyond, a meadow lies,
Where calmness rests beneath blue skies.
The balance sways, it tips, it turns,
A flicker bright, a steady burn.
The noise may claw, it will not win,
The silence waits to draw me in.
Each thought that pounds, each voice that calls,
Begins to fade as stillness falls.
Between the chaos and the peace,
A quiet tension brings release.
The edge of silence hums so near,
A gentle place, my heart's frontier.

The Balance of Air

The air is thick with shouts and cries,
A swirling storm of endless skies.
It pushes hard, it pulls me thin,
A noisy tempest deep within.
Yet in the gale, a calm takes hold,
A space untouched, serene and bold.
The eye of storms, a sacred land,
Where stillness holds me in its hand.
Between the chaos and the rest,
The balance lives within my chest.
A breath, a pause, a moment's grace,
Creates a wide and peaceful space.
The noise will come, the stillness stay,
In balance, I will find my way.

The Call of Both Worlds

Noise calls loud, it wants my all,
It drags me into its wild sprawl.
Yet stillness calls, a gentler sound,
A quiet place where peace is found.
Between their voices, I must tread,
One pulls my heart, the other, my head.
The noise ignites, it drives, it fuels,
The stillness mends, it calms, it cools.
I walk the line they carve in air,
A tightrope thin, a path laid bare.
And in their dance, I come to see,
Both have their truths, both set me free.
The balance lives where they both meet,
A harmony both loud and sweet.

The Rhythm of Rest and Rush

The rush of life, it fills my veins,
It pounds my pulse, it strains my reins.
Yet in the rhythm, a pause appears,
A space to rest, to shed my fears.
The noise propels, it pushes fast,
But stillness lingers, built to last.
Each beat a drive, each rest a gift,
A balance found in every shift.
Between the rush and quiet stay,
I find the path, I make my way.
The rhythm guides, it calms, it stirs,
Through every pause, my spirit concurs.
Both rush and rest are mine to take,
A harmony for balance's sake.

The Silent Answer

The questions rise, the doubts grow loud,
A mental storm, a restless crowd.
The noise demands, it seeks control,
It tears apart my fragile soul.
But through the din, a silence speaks,
Its tone is soft, its voice unique.
No answers bold, no shouts or cries,
Just quiet truth beneath the skies.
Between the noise and silence's pull,
I find my center, calm and full.
No need for shouting, no need for fight,
The silent answer shines its light.
And in its glow, I come to know,
The balance found will help me grow.

The Space Between

In the space between each sound and word,
There lives a peace that goes unheard.
The quiet hum of stillness waits,
A place where noise evaporates.
The chaos hums, it fills the day,
It pulls my thoughts, it makes me sway.
Yet stillness answers, calm and clear,
A place where I can hold the near.
Between the two, a balance grows,
A gentle stream that softly flows.
Both noise and silence play their part,
To stir the mind and heal the heart.
In this space, I choose to stay,
Where balance guides my every way.

A Crack in the Dark

Through shadows thick, through endless night,
There shines a single shard of light.
Its glow is soft, its reach is small,
Yet it begins to break the wall.
The darkness trembles, it starts to wane,
As light pours through like healing rain.
Each ray, a truth, each beam, a guide,
To lead me where my fears collide.
No need to run, no need to hide,
For in this light, my heart can bide.
It whispers hope, it carves a way,
Through night to greet the coming day.
A crack in the dark, so bright, so true,
The light begins, it sees me through.

The Splintered Ray

A splintered ray, so faint, so shy,
Pierces clouds that hide the sky.
It doesn't scream, it doesn't fight,
But softly scatters shards of light.
Each gleam a thought, each spark a word,
A song of truth that goes unheard.
The shadows twist, they shrink, they fall,
As light breaks through the heavy pall.
Though small at first, the glow expands,
It stretches wide, it takes my hands.
It lifts me up, it shows the way,
A spark that births the dawn of day.
Oh, splintered ray, you save my sight,
And guide me through the endless night.

The Light That Lingers

The night holds tight, it cloaks the air,
It whispers fears, it plants despair.
Yet in its grasp, a light remains,
A shard that cuts through all the chains.
Its glow is subtle, soft and near,
A quiet voice that silences fear.
No shadow hides, no dark conceals,
The truth this glowing shard reveals.
It lingers here, it does not flee,
A promise held eternally.
It waits for eyes that dare to see,
The beauty of its clarity.
Oh, lingering light, you hold me fast,
A beacon bright until the last.

A Spark Amidst the Shade

Amidst the shade, so deep, so wide,
A tiny spark begins to guide.
It flickers faint, it trembles soft,
Yet draws me to its glowing loft.
The shadows dance, they writhe, they fall,
But light begins to touch it all.
Each spark a key, each gleam a door,
To lead me to the truth once more.
It doesn't blaze, it doesn't burn,
But softly calls, "It's time to learn."
And as I follow, step by step,
The shadows lose the hold they kept.
Oh, spark of light, so small, so bright,
You turn my dark to boundless sight.

The First Gleam

The first gleam pierces through the veil,
A quiet force, so slight, so frail.
It doesn't shout, it doesn't fight,
But plants the seed of coming light.
Its beam reveals the hidden truth,
The shadows' weight, the lies of youth.
Each angle shifts, each corner bends,
As clarity begins, ascends.
The gleam grows bold, it carves a way,
To turn the night into the day.
It doesn't fade, it doesn't cease,
It fills the heart with steady peace.
Oh, first gleam, how your truth does grow,
A light that leads where I must go.

The Breaking Dawn

The dawn arrives, its shards of gold,
Break through the dark, the shadows fold.
Each ray ignites, each line reveals,
The hidden wounds the heart conceals.
The light, though soft, begins to spread,
To clear the paths where darkness tread.
It warms the air, it fills the space,
It draws me to its healing grace.
Each shard a truth, each beam a guide,
To navigate the fears inside.
The dawn, though slow, will always come,
To end the night and bring the sun.
Oh, breaking dawn, your shards I claim,
To heal my heart and spark my flame.

A Shard of Knowing

A shard of knowing strikes my mind,
It cuts through doubts and thoughts confined.
Its edge is sharp, its glow is pure,
A sudden truth, a sacred cure.
The darkness flinches, pulls away,
As insight floods the lightless grey.
Each glimmer brings a spark of hope,
Each moment clears the tangled rope.
It doesn't fade, it doesn't flee,
It stays to guide, it sets me free.
This shard of knowing, fierce and bright,
Transforms my fears with quiet might.
Oh, shard of light, my heart you save,
A fearless guide, both strong and brave.

Through the Cracks

Through cracks, the light begins to pour,
It slips through walls, it finds the floor.
It glides along, it fills the space,
It chases shadows from their place.
The cracks may widen, gaps may grow,
But light reveals what I must know.
It doesn't rush, it doesn't shout,
But clears the haze of fear and doubt.
Each shard that gleams, each ray that glows,
Unveils the truth the shadow chose.
And as the light begins to climb,
The cracks dissolve, the walls decline.
Oh, through the cracks, your light has won,
A boundless path where I can run.

A Whisper of Light

The dark holds court, it reigns the night,
Yet through it comes a whisper of light.
So faint, so soft, it dares to show,
The truth beneath the shadow's glow.
Its whisper grows, it fills the air,
It spreads its warmth, it plants its care.
Each gentle flicker clears the space,
And brings me closer to its grace.
The shadows quake, they start to fade,
The whisper's light begins to aid.
It doesn't stop, it doesn't tire,
Its glow a quiet, burning fire.
Oh, whispering light, your truth is near,
You lift my heart, you calm my fear.

The Splinter of Hope

A splinter sharp, a shard of glass,
Cuts through the dark where fears amass.
It shines, it hums, it starts to grow,
A beacon where no light should show.
Its edges gleam, its glow expands,
It reaches out with steady hands.
The dark retreats, it can't compete,
With hope that rises, strong and sweet.
The splinter's power doesn't wane,
It gathers strength to heal the pain.
Through broken lines, the light takes flight,
A promise held within its sight.
Oh, splinter of hope, your glow I claim,
To light my soul, to fan my flame.

Fragments of Fire

The fire breaks, its fragments fly,
Across the darkened, endless sky.
Each spark a light, each light a guide,
To pierce the night where fears reside.
The fragments burn, they blaze, they gleam,
A scattered truth, a vivid dream.
They do not fade, they do not fail,
They carve a path through shadow's veil.
Each ember speaks of strength unseen,
Of clarity where pain had been.
And as they spark, the dark gives way,
To welcome in the break of day.
Oh, fragments of fire, your truth I see,
A scattered light that sets me free.

The Shard of Dawn

The shard of dawn ignites the air,
It casts away despair's cruel snare.
Each golden beam, a lifeline pure,
A light to guide, a path secure.
It whispers softly, "Here you'll find,
A place to rest, a peace of mind."
The darkness bends, it starts to break,
The dawn begins, the soul awake.
Each shard a promise, bright and kind,
To lead me from the dark I find.
And as it grows, the night will flee,
Revealing all that's meant to be.
Oh, shard of dawn, your light I hold,
A truth more precious than purest gold.

The Rooted Moment

Beneath the noise, beneath the rush,
Lies a moment, calm and lush.
No past to haunt, no future chase,
Just the stillness of this place.
The earth beneath, the sky above,
The steady pulse of life and love.
Each breath a thread, each pause a tie,
To anchor me as time drifts by.
The present hums, its voice is low,
A song of now, a gentle glow.
No need to reach, no need to roam,
This grounded space becomes my home.
Oh, rooted now, I stand, I see,
The gift of life, eternally free.

The Ground Beneath

The ground beneath, so firm, so sure,
Holds every step I take, secure.
Its quiet strength, its solid grace,
A steady presence, a sacred space.
Each moment lands, it doesn't flee,
A truth unfolding endlessly.
No fleeting thoughts, no future fears,
Just here and now, where all appears.
The ground holds all, it doesn't change,
No need to search, no need to range.
It waits for me to plant my feet,
To find the now, to make it sweet.
Oh, ground beneath, you keep me whole,
A timeless anchor for my soul.

Breath by Breath

Each breath a gift, so soft, so true,
A quiet bridge that guides me through.
No race to run, no clock to beat,
Just air that moves, a rhythm sweet.
Inhale the sky, exhale the night,
The breath aligns, it sets things right.
Each cycle brings the moment near,
A space unburdened, calm and clear.
The breath connects, it doesn't stray,
It roots me deep, it lights the way.
No need for more, no need for less,
The breath becomes my sweet caress.
Oh, breath of now, my steadfast guide,
With you, I live, with you, I bide.

The Eternal Now

Time moves fast, it doesn't stay,
Yet the present holds its quiet sway.
A place untouched by rushing streams,
A home for hearts, a field of dreams.
The past may call, the future shout,
But here and now, there is no doubt.
Its stillness hums, its peace is wide,
A timeless space where truths reside.
No grasping hands, no fleeting chase,
Just steady breath, a grounded grace.
The eternal now, so calm, so clear,
Becomes a place where all is near.
Oh, present moment, vast and free,
You hold the world and anchor me.

A Pause Between

Between the noise, a silence grows,
A pause where all my spirit knows.
It doesn't clamour, doesn't flee,
But waits for me to simply be.
Each pause a chance to settle deep,
To plant the seeds that stillness keeps.
No rushing tides, no restless air,
Just quiet moments free from care.
The pause expands, it holds the light,
It balances both dark and bright.
Between the chaos and the calm,
It offers peace, a healing balm.
Oh, sacred pause, you draw me in,
A refuge where new life begins.

The Steady Hand

The present waits, a steady hand,
To hold me firm, to help me stand.
It doesn't falter, doesn't stray,
But guides me through the longest day.
No wandering thoughts, no endless streams,
Just open skies and quiet dreams.
The hand extends, it says, "Be here,
The now is where all truths appear."
I take its grip, I feel its strength,
It grounds my soul through time and length.
The steady hand, so firm, so kind,
Anchors me to the weightless mind.
Oh, present guide, you lead me true,
Each moment born anew with you.

The Weight of Now

The now is light, yet full and vast,
It holds no future, keeps no past.
Its weight is not a burdened hold,
But solid truth, both calm and bold.
It asks for nothing, gives me all,
A steady ground, a gentle call.
No spinning wheels, no racing thought,
Just simple peace that can't be bought.
The weight of now, it centres me,
It roots my heart, it sets me free.
No greater gift, no deeper place,
Than living in its present grace.
Oh, weight of now, I feel your pull,
A perfect moment, vast and full.

The Present Horizon

The present stretches wide and far,
A horizon bright, a guiding star.
It doesn't fade, it doesn't flee,
But waits with quiet certainty.
Each moment glows, it doesn't hide,
It opens paths where dreams reside.
No rush, no race, no time to lose,
Just endless choices left to choose.
The present hums, it softly sings,
A melody of simple things.
The now unfolds, it lets me see,
The beauty of eternity.
Oh, present horizon, calm and wide,
You hold my heart, my truth, my guide.

Roots in the Now

The now holds roots, so strong, so deep,
They ground my soul, they let me keep.
Each moment born, each breath I take,
A sacred tie I cannot fake.
The roots don't falter, don't give way,
They hold me firm through night and day.
No future storms, no past's regret,
Can shake the truths these roots beget.
They weave through soil, they steady all,
They catch me when I fear to fall.
The now provides, it doesn't flee,
Its roots entwined eternally.
Oh, present roots, your strength I claim,
To ground my heart, to stake my name.

The Stillness Speaks

The stillness speaks in gentle tones,
It echoes through my skin and bones.
It tells me here is where I'll find,
A calmer heart, a quieter mind.
The noise may rise, the winds may scream,
Yet stillness holds a steady beam.
Its voice is soft, its pull is true,
It lights the path I'm walking through.
In stillness, all becomes so clear,
Each truth, each love, each moment near.
It doesn't fight, it doesn't shout,
It simply shows what life's about.
Oh, stillness deep, your voice I hear,
You guide me home, you keep me near.

The Anchored Soul

The soul, it drifts, it often sways,
Through endless tides and winding ways.
Yet in the now, it finds its place,
A quiet calm, a rooted space.
No waves can pull, no winds can tear,
The anchored soul is always there.
It doesn't seek, it doesn't yearn,
But takes the time to breathe, to learn.
Its anchor holds through every tide,
A steadfast truth that won't subside.
In every moment, wide and small,
The anchored soul receives it all.
Oh, anchored soul, your peace I crave,
A timeless guide, so strong, so brave.

The Gift of Now

The now is rare, a fleeting gift,
It doesn't wait, it doesn't drift.
Yet in its grasp, the world unfolds,
A treasure vast, more rich than gold.
It asks for little, gives so much,
A grounding breath, a healing touch.
No need to hurry, no need to chase,
The now will always hold its place.
Each moment here, each second free,
Brings endless joy and clarity.
The past can't hold, the future flee,
For in the now, I learn to be.
Oh, gift of now, so bright, so true,
You guide my steps, my heart, my view.

The Flow of Ease

Words like water softly flow,
A gentle stream where stillness grows.
They carve a path through tangled thought,
And bring the peace my soul has sought.
Each phrase a ripple, calm and true,
Each sound a wave that pulls me through.
The current hums, the tension fades,
The mind unwinds in soothing shades.
No need to fight, no need to stay,
The water knows the perfect way.
It carries me where I belong,
A quiet place where I grow strong.

A River's Song

The river sings in tender tones,
A lullaby of shifting stones.
Its words, so smooth, so clear, so kind,
Flow softly through my weary mind.
It asks for nothing, gives me all,
It catches every tear that falls.
The doubts dissolve, the fears are gone,
Its soothing current pulls me on.
Each word, a note, each line, a sound,
A melody where peace is found.
Oh, river's song, you heal, you mend,
You guide me to my journey's end.

The Whispering Stream

A stream that whispers, soft and low,
Reveals the truths I long to know.
Its voice is faint, yet strong and clear,
A balm for hearts that ache with fear.
It winds through valleys, hills, and trees,
It dances gently with the breeze.
Each word it speaks, a healing kiss,
A fleeting moment of quiet bliss.
The stream reminds, with every turn,
That peace is something we must learn.
Its waters wash my spirit clean,
And leave me calm, serene, unseen.

Liquid Light

The words, like liquid light, descend,
To warm the heart, to softly mend.
They shimmer bright, they catch the sun,
And soothe the battles I have won.
They trickle gently, line by line,
They cleanse the shadows in my mind.
No force they bring, no fight they take,
Just quiet clarity they make.
Each drop, a thought, each phrase, a spark,
That lights the path within the dark.
Oh, liquid light, your flow I claim,
To find my peace, to ease my flame.

Waves of Wisdom

The waves roll in, they kiss the sand,
A rhythmic truth, a steady hand.
Their words are soft, yet strong and sure,
They whisper wisdom, calm, and pure.
Each wave dissolves the pain I bear,
Each cresting thought, a breath of air.
The ocean speaks, its voice so kind,
It clears the clutter from my mind.
It doesn't hurry, doesn't race,
It moves with patience, love, and grace.
Oh, waves of wisdom, guide me home,
Through seas of peace where I can roam.

The Calm Cascade

The cascade falls, its silver stream,
A liquid hope, a lucid dream.
Its sound, a balm, its touch, a prayer,
It lifts my worries from the air.
Each drop a word, each line a touch,
A soothing flow I crave so much.
It shapes the stone, it clears the way,
And carries all my fear away.
The cascade hums, it sings, it mends,
It turns my chaos into friends.
Oh, flowing fall, your truth I find,
A gentle stream that soothes my mind.

Ripples of Clarity

A ripple spreads, its circle wide,
It touches hearts, it soothes inside.
Its source unknown, its reach so vast,
It carries moments meant to last.
Each ripple, calm, each movement clear,
It washes doubt, it draws me near.
The ripples flow, they softly break,
And leave a stillness in their wake.
Oh, rippled mind, so vast, so free,
Your gentle waves bring clarity.
The pond reflects the truths I seek,
A mirror deep, profound, unique.

Water's Embrace

The water holds, it doesn't press,
A cradle soft, a firm caress.
Its arms are wide, its touch is light,
It soothes the mind through day and night.
It asks no questions, needs no proof,
It bends to shape, it tells the truth.
The current flows, the heart is calm,
Its rhythm acts as healing balm.
The water whispers, "Let it go,
Release the weight, just let it flow."
Oh, water's touch, your truth I crave,
A soft embrace, a path to save.

The Stream of Mind

The mind, a stream, it twists, it turns,
Through every bend, a lesson burns.
Its waters rush, its current pulls,
Yet in its flow, the heart grows full.
Each word it carries, soft or loud,
Becomes a mist, a calming cloud.
The stream does not hold tight or keep,
It flows through dreams, through fears, through sleep.
It doesn't stop, it doesn't stay,
But gently clears the cluttered way.
Oh, stream of mind, your flow I find,
A guiding path, both strong and kind.

Rainfall of Words

The rain descends, its song begins,
It cleanses all my hidden sins.
Each drop, a word, each splash, a phrase,
A gentle hymn through cloudy days.
The rain's embrace, so soft, so cool,
Transforms the heart, becomes its pool.
The world it feeds, the soul it fills,
A tranquil calm, a quiet thrill.
It falls without, it heals within,
A soothing touch on weary skin.
Oh, rain of words, fall steady, free,
And let your clarity drench me.

The Well Within

Within my soul, a well resides,
Its waters deep, its flow abides.
It holds no weight, it keeps no pain,
Its truth a sweet and endless gain.
I draw its words with every breath,
Each one a guard against regret.
Its waters rise, they kiss the air,
A hidden source beyond compare.
The well within, its flow so pure,
It offers peace, it whispers cure.
Oh, endless well, your depths I find,
A stream of solace for my mind.

Ocean of Stillness

The ocean waits, its vast expanse,
A timeless place where hearts can dance.
Its waves are calm, its waters clear,
A boundless space that draws me near.
Each thought dissolves beneath its touch,
Each doubt becomes a thing of much.
The ocean speaks, it doesn't shout,
Its whispers melt my fear and doubt.
Its ebb and flow, its endless song,
Has held my heart, has made me strong.
Oh, ocean still, your truth I see,
A calming tide that carries me.

The Gentle Shore

Come rest beside the gentle shore,
Where waves erase what came before.
The tide will carry all you fear,
And leave you lighter, calm, and clear.
The sand beneath, the air above,
Holds whispers soft of care and love.
Release the weight, let go the bind,
And feel the peace you're sure to find.
The shore knows well the pain you keep,
It soothes your heart, it lets you weep.
Let waves remind you of the way,
To let life flow and greet the day.

A Breath to Begin

Inhale the air, so cool, so light,
Exhale the weight that binds you tight.
Let every breath become a guide,
To lead you where calm waters bide.
No need to hold, no need to fight,
The breath will bring your soul to flight.
Its rhythm hums, it eases pain,
It softens sorrow, clears the strain.
A single breath can build a place,
Of gentle stillness, quiet grace.
So breathe and know, through rise and fall,
The breath will soothe, it answers all.

The River of Time

The river flows, it will not stay,
It carries all that clogs your way.
No need to swim, no need to hold,
The river knows its course is bold.
Let go the branches, let them fall,
The river's arms will catch it all.
It bends and winds, it doesn't tire,
It calms your heart, it lifts you higher.
Each passing wave, a fleeting thought,
Each current clears what life has wrought.
Oh, trust the river's gentle pace,
And find within a healing space.

A Pause for Peace

The world may call, it moves so fast,
Yet peace resides where stillness lasts.
A single pause, a moment's rest,
Can ease the weight upon your chest.
No need to chase, no need to flee,
Just let the moment cradle thee.
Its silence speaks, its touch is kind,
It clears the clutter in your mind.
The pause is simple, soft, and true,
It doesn't ask too much of you.
In pausing now, the calm will grow,
And guide your steps wherever you go.

Through the Window of Now

The present waits, so calm, so wide,
A window open deep inside.
The past may call, the future scream,
But now is where the soul can dream.
No shadow lingers in its glow,
No racing thoughts disturb its flow.
It simply holds, it simply stays,
A refuge from life's hurried ways.
Step through the frame, let worries fade,
And feel the peace the now has made.
The present's gift is yours to keep,
A place of still, a tranquil deep.

The Ground Beneath You

The earth below, so firm, so true,
Holds steady ground beneath your shoe.
It doesn't waver, doesn't break,
It's here with every step you take.
Let its presence anchor you,
Through skies of grey or shades of blue.
It doesn't judge, it doesn't blame,
It holds your weight without a claim.
Feel its strength, so quiet, sure,
A constant balm, a steady cure.
The ground beneath reminds you so,
That peace is here, wherever you go.

The Quiet Sky

Look to the sky, so vast, so free,
A gentle, calming canopy.
Its blues and whites, its endless space,
Remind you of life's soothing grace.
The clouds may drift, the winds may rise,
But stillness lives within those skies.
A sky so wide, it doesn't hold,
Yet offers strength so calm, so bold.
Let its expanse clear out your mind,
And leave the fear of life behind.
The quiet sky will always stay,
A friend to guide you on your way.

The Light Within

There's light inside, so soft, so warm,
It shields you through life's fiercest storm.
It doesn't dim, it doesn't fade,
It glows in shadows darkly laid.
Its fire burns when hope seems lost,
It guides you through each fear you've crossed.
No matter how the world may spin,
The steady light is yours within.
So close your eyes and feel its glow,
A truth you've carried, yet may not know.
This inner flame will see you through,
A source of strength for all you do.

Disclaimer

The poems in this book are intended to inspire self-reflection, mindfulness, and emotional clarity. They are not a substitute for professional mental health support or therapy. While the words may offer comfort or perspective, they should not replace advice or treatment from qualified mental health professionals.

If you are experiencing persistent mental health challenges, overwhelming stress, or emotional distress, please reach out to a licensed therapist, counsellor, or medical professional. Your well-being is important, and help is available.

This book is a creative expression, and the interpretations of the poems may vary for each reader. Take what resonates with you, and let the rest gently pass.